POWER POEMS

for small humans

Curated by S. Bear Bergman

Drawn by Kai

Colored by Quinn

HOW TO use this book

Some poems to learn and remember
If you should happen to ever
Be in a hard spot
With hard thoughts.
These poets and writers have saved —
For when you need to be brave —
Some ideas for how
To remember your power.

Written by Andrea Gibson

Illustrated by Ashley Wong

I don't know the future
and it's okay that I don't know.
The sky was expecting sunshine
then my tongue was catching snow.

I can handle whatever comes my way.
I can handle what doesn't too.
Maybe cows expected to chirp like birds
Then HOLY COW! They MOOOOO'd!

I come from Black Freedom Fighters across 7 seas
Queen Nanny Maroon, Marie Joseph Angelique
and magnificent Marsha P.

I walk with power carrying their legacy.
I was born to be revolutionary!

Written by LeRoi Newbold

Illustrated by Adee Roberson

Written by Liz Morgan

Illustrated by Kit Lang

Some families are big, some families are small,
Some families have two dads, and some none at all.

I could have a twin, I could be an only,
Or so many siblings I never get lonely.

I might look like my parents, or be different colors
Or me and my siblings could have different mothers.

We may not be perfect or always agree
But the love that we share makes my family tree!

it happens when we least expect –
and mostly, we don't mean to.

we use sharp words, or throw our fists
or say something not true.

it's easy, then, to run away
or hide! but friend, I promise:

to say, "I'm sorry I hurt you,"
is right and brave and honest.

Written by Kai Cheng Thom

Illustrated by Aria Feliciano

When I have to try new things,
I do my best imaginings.

Trying is my special skill.
If I worry, I'll try still.

Things don't have to be perfect to be great. Let's just try and celebrate!

Written by Theresa I. Soto

Illustrated by Zoraida Ingles

Written by Jillian Christmas

Illustrated by Sonja John

my anger sometimes starts as an earthquake
down in the pit of my gut

a wriggling   trembling   terrible thing
I just wish that I could hush up

a twisting   uncomfortable   troubling ache
that can't help but bubble and pop

and every time that I try to speak   it yells
over each word I talk

I've tried to ignore it   or push it way down
but none of those tricks seem to work for too long

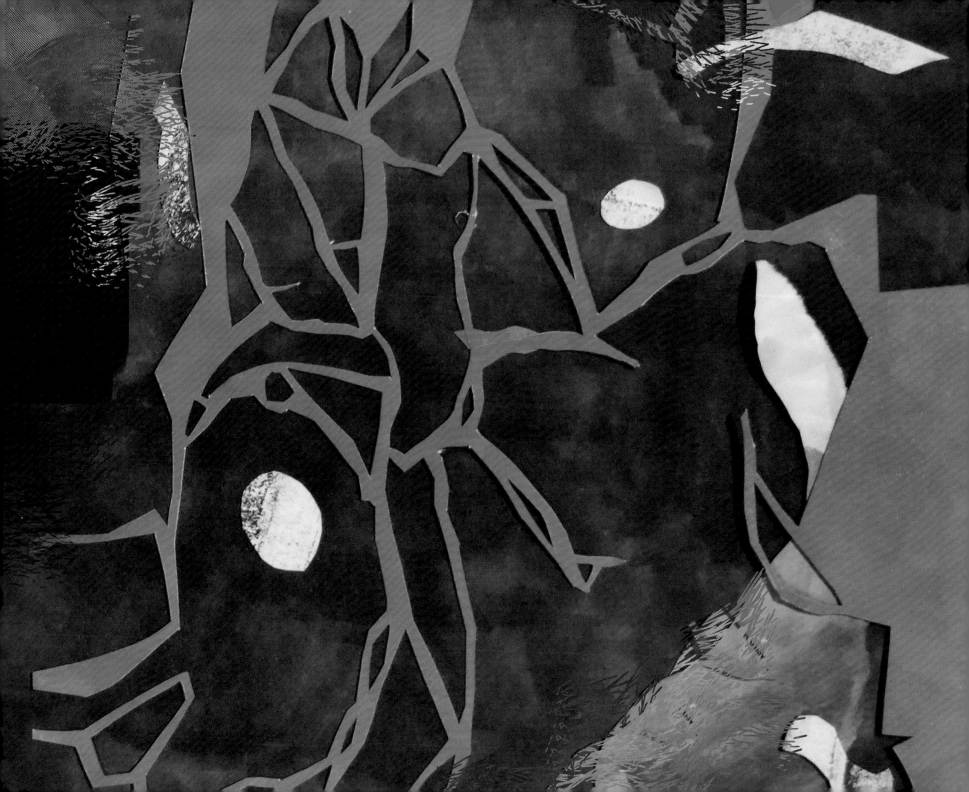

I soothed them and cooed them and even
boo-hooed them   until they were almost all gone

I stomped them and clapped them and wrote them
and tapped them and told them to people who understood

when I looked at my anger again in the mirror
I found it was special and good

my anger had not been coming around to hurt me
but to tell me that things weren't quite right

once I looked at my anger and listened and loved it
it practically flew out of sight

my anger was just like the honk of a siren
checking in that I was ok

so long as I notice and ask what it's thinking
it has no more reason to stay.

so today I am making a friend of my anger
and thanking it for all that it knows

And when I don't need it   I'll try not to feed it
and wave it goodbye as it goes

Are you a girl or a boy?
There is no one else like me!

Are you a girl or a boy?
In my dreams, everyone calls me by
my right name.

Are you a girl or a boy?
In the future it won't matter

Are you a girl or a boy?
This is the future, the future is now.

Written by Andrea Jenkins

Illustrated by Sofia Misenheimer

Trust myself first.
Self-respect is most deserved.
Even when I'm lonely,
I am filled with love and worth.

Written by Britta Badour

Illustrated by Christina Ogbotiti

SORROW

JOY

HAPPY

SAD

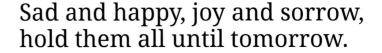

HOPE

Sad and happy, joy and sorrow,
hold them all until tomorrow.

If it helps, mix them up
make *jorrow* in a pretty cup

Salty, sweet and bitter too,
add some hopeful to my brew.

It's hard to hold and that's okay.
A new chance comes with each new day.

JORROW

Written by Jen Goldberg

Illustrated by Brit Ouchida

Let my surroundings comfort me, and soak in the air,
Feel the earth ground me, release my despair.
Feel calm, and at peace, and totally balanced.
I know I am strong; I can face any challenge.

Written by Amir Rabiyah

Illustrated by Paulino Meija

OPEN SPACE

for dreaming

Now it's your turn:
write down a poem
or just some thoughts
to help you remember your power.

What do people who love me say that makes me feel peaceful and powerful?
What do I say to help others feel that way? What do I wish someone *would* say?

_____

_____

_____

_____

_____

_____

My Poem

_____

_____

_____

_____

_____

_____

_____